Th Little Tiger book belongs to:

_____ _____

_____ _____

                                    2

_____ _____

For Mum, Dad and Val ~ SP

Publications
Centre, 189 Munster Road, London SW6 6AW
www.littletigerpress.com
First published in Great Britain 2009
This edition published 2010
Text copyright © Magi Publications 2009
Illustrations copyright © Simon Prescott 2009
Simon Prescott has asserted his right to be identified as the illustrator
of this work under the Copyright, Designs and Patents Act, 1988
A CIP catalogue record for this book is available from the British Library
All rights reserved • ISBN 978-1-84506-760-1
Printed in China • 10 9 8 7 6 5 4 3 2 1

Flat 2b,
1091 Stilton Row,
City Heights,
Mouseville

Dear Country Mouse,

Please come and stay in the
city with me. There's so much
to do and so much to see.
You will love it!
See you soon.

Love, City Mouse X

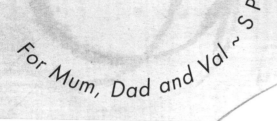

Small Mouse
BIG CITY

Simon Prescott

LITTLE TIGER PRESS
London

Country Mouse was leaving his quiet little home. He was going to the Big City.

His heart raced, as the countryside swept by in a blur of leafy green.

The city took his breath away.

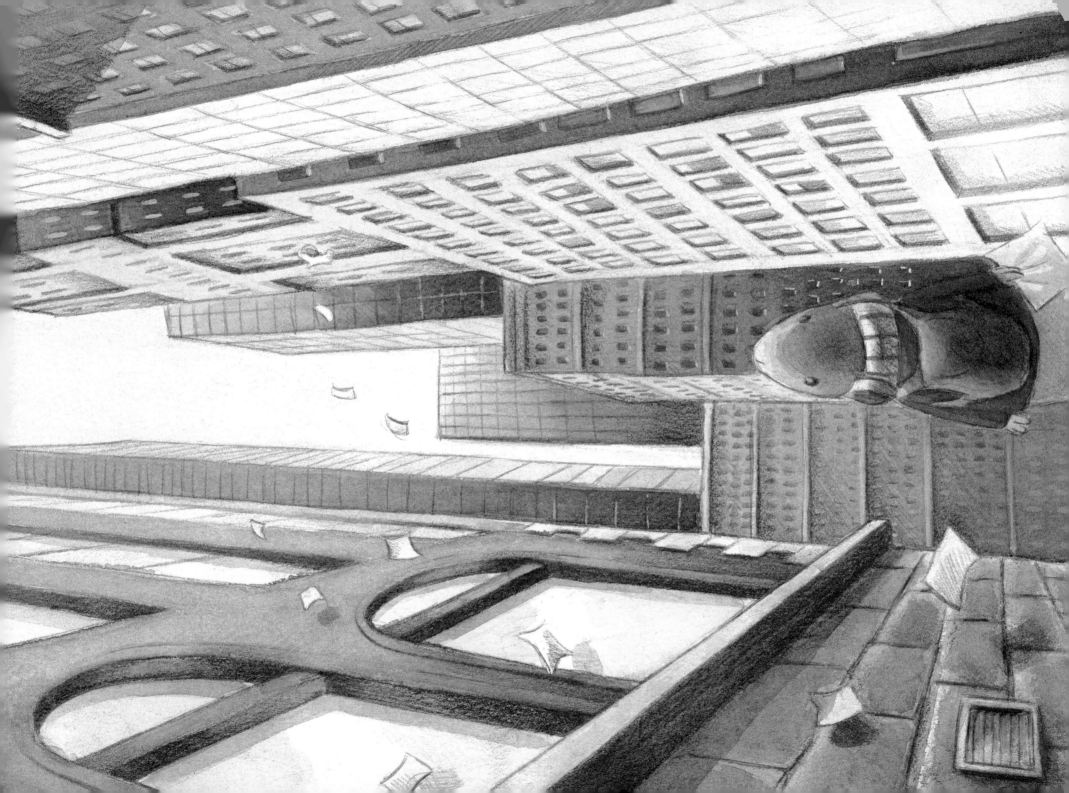

There were so many people . . .

. . . but no one stopped to show him the way.

Country Mouse was on his own.

And the streets all looked the same . . .

strange . . .

dark . . .

...and **dangerous!**

He needed a friend – fast!
And he showed up just in time.

Suddenly the city
didn't feel so strange.

"You'll love it here,"
said City Mouse.

And he did!

The city was amazing!

The city was intoxicating!

The city was magnificent!

But when Country Mouse gazed across
the rooftops and saw the green hills of
his home, he began to feel sad.

"I miss my countryside," he said, and he told his friend all about it – how beautiful it was, how peaceful.

He loved City Mouse
and he loved the city.

But it was time to go home.

Country Mouse lay out on the soft, green grass and smiled. "It's good to be back!" he said. "There's just no place like home."

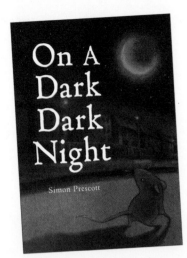

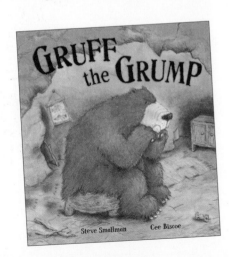